Dear Parent:

Your child's love of reading starts here!

Every child learns to read in a different way and at his or her own speed. Some go back and forth between reading levels and read favorite books again and again. Others read through each level in order. You can help your young reader improve and become more confident by encouraging his or her own interests and abilities. From books your child reads with you to the first books he or she reads alone, there are I Can Read Books for every stage of reading:

SHARED READING
Basic language, word repetition, and whimsical illustrations, ideal for sharing with your emergent reader

BEGINNING READING
Short sentences, familiar words, and simple concepts for children eager to read on their own

READING WITH HELP
Engaging stories, longer sentences, and language play for developing readers

READING ALONE
Complex plots, challenging vocabulary, and high-interest topics for the independent reader

I Can Read Books have introduced children to the joy of reading since 1957. Featuring award-winning authors and illustrators and a fabulous cast of beloved characters, I Can Read Books set the standard for beginning readers.

A lifetime of discovery begins with the magical words **"I Can Read!"**

Visit www.icanread.com for information on enriching your child's reading experience.

BEGINNING
1
READING
I Can Read!
Pinkalicious®
Dragon to the Rescue

To Echo
—V.K.

The author gratefully acknowledges
the artistic and editorial contributions of
Daniel Griffo and Jacqueline Resnick.

Based on the HarperCollins book *Pinkalicious* written by
Victoria Kann and Elizabeth Kann, illustrated by Victoria Kann

For information address HarperCollins Children's Books, a division of HarperCollins Publishers,
195 Broadway, New York, NY 10007.
www.icanread.com

Library of Congress Control Number: 2019933061
ISBN 978-0-06-284042-4 (trade bdg.)—ISBN 978-0-06-284041-7 (pbk.)

19 20 21 22 23 LSCC 10 9 8 7 6 5 4 3
❖
First Edition

by Victoria Kann

HARPER
An Imprint of HarperCollins*Publishers*

"Welcome, happy campers!"
I said to my friends.
They were at my house
for a campfire party!

"Let's look at the stars!" I said.

"What do you see?"

"I see the Big Dipper," said Alison.

"I see a dragon!" Peter said.

The wind began to blow.
“I can feel the dragon’s breath,”
Molly said with a giggle.

The wind blew harder.

Suddenly, it blew out our fire!

Alison grabbed my hand.

"Now it's really dark," she said.

"Should we go inside?" Molly asked.

“If only our starry dragon

could light the fire,” Peter said.

“He can’t,” I said.

“But I know a dragon who can!”

"We need Gertie the dragon!"

I said to my friends.

"How do we find her?" Peter asked.

"We have to visualize her!" I said.

"Then she'll appear."

We closed our eyes.

"I can picture her.

She is big and pink!" Molly said.

"She's flying through the stars!"

Alison said.

"And over the moon!" said Peter.

"Hello," said a voice.

It was our pinkatastic dragon friend!

"We did it!" Peter gasped.

"Hooray!" Molly cheered.

"Welcome to our campfire,"

Alison said.

"Ooh, I love campfires," Gertie said.
"But where is the fire?"
"The wind blew it out," I said.
"Can you relight it?"

Gertie breathed a big flame.

"Thanks!" Molly said.

"Now we can tell campfire stories,"

Alison said.

“Let’s play the story game!” I said.

“What’s that?” Peter asked.

“We tell a story all together,”

I explained.

“We each take a turn adding a line.”

"I'll start!" Molly said.

"It was a dark and stormy night,"

she said in her spookiest voice.

"The trees creaked," Peter continued.

"The thunder got louder," Alison said.

"And louder, until . . ."

"BOOM!" I shouted.

"AHHHH!" Gertie screamed.

She flapped her wings so hard

that she snuffed out the fire.

“Oops,” Gertie squeaked.

“Scary stories scare me!”

“Dragons get scared?” Peter asked.

“Everyone gets scared sometimes,”

Gertie said.

“Speaking of scared,” Alison said,

“it’s really, really dark.”

So I asked Gertie,

“Could you light the fire again?”

Gertie breathed deeply,
but no flames came out.
“I’m sorry,” she said.
“I’m too scared to breathe fire.”
“My mom gives me a bear hug
when I get scared,” Alison said.

“Maybe Gertie needs a dragon hug!”
Molly said.
“Great idea!” I said.

We gave Gertie a big hug.

“Do you feel better?” I asked.

“I feel very loved,” Gertie said.

She took a deep breath.

No flames came out.

“I guess I’m still a bit scared,”

Gertie said.

Suddenly, I heard a rumble.

“Is that thunder?” Molly asked.

“Is that wind?” Peter asked.

“No,” Alison said.

“It’s Gertie’s tummy!”

“I get hungry when I’m scared,”

Gertie said.

“Don’t worry,” I said.

“I have the perfect dragon food!”

I waved a pink marshmallow
under Gertie's nose.
Her nose twitched.
"I wish we had a fire
to roast these marshmallows,"
Peter said loudly.

“We could make s’mores!” I said.
“Did someone say s’mores?”
Gertie asked.

Gertie breathed a big flame.

"You did it!" Alison said.

"You saved our campfire!" Molly said.

"You're very brave," Peter told her.

"Three cheers for Gertie!" I said.

"I'd prefer three marshmallows,"

Gertie said.

She breathed another flame.

It roasted our marshmallows!

"I'm glad you came to our campfire,"
I told Gertie.
"Me too," Gertie said.
"Everything is S'MORE fun
with friends!"